The Author

Stephanie Dagg lives in Innishannon, County Cork.

She is a mother of two children, Benjamin and Caitlín, and has been writing stories ever since she was a child. Originally from Suffolk in England, she moved to Cork in 1992.

Contents

Chapter 1
Off to a Bad Start

Lucy stood on the doorstep with Dad and her little brother, Michael, waving goodbye to Mum as the taxi whisked her away down the drive. Mum was off to a business conference for two days. It would be Friday night before she would be back. That seemed like a long time to Lucy. It seemed an eternity to Michael, who was only two. He started howling.

Meanwhile Dad was in charge. He'd taken some days off work to 'hold the fort' as he liked to say. Trouble was, he didn't hold it very well! The last time Mum had gone away on a business trip, Lucy and Michael had lived on toasted cheese sandwiches as that was nearly all that poor Dad could make.

Dad also liked to make curries, but Michael and Lucy did not like curries. *And* he'd managed to lock them all out of the house one evening. *And* once he'd taken Lucy to swimming instead of taking her to ballet.

Lucy sighed. Things tended to go wrong when Dad was in charge. The next two days without Mum were bound to be eventful.

'Come on!' said Dad when the taxi was out of sight. 'Time to get ready for school, Lucy. We must make sure we don't miss the school bus.'

(Oh yes, they'd been late for the bus the last time Mum was away!)

The children trooped back inside and headed upstairs to the bathroom to get washed. Michael was still snivelling.

'Hush now, Mikey,' soothed Dad. 'Here, have a sweetie to cheer you up.'

Dad delved in his dressing gown pocket and dug out a rather furry piece of chocolate.

Oh Dad!

He'd obviously been prepared for tears! The chocolate successfully stopped Michael's snivelling – for the moment, anyway.

'OK Lucy, get dressed first and then washed,' announced Dad.

'Mum always makes me do it the other way round,' protested Lucy.

'Does she?' said Dad, surprised. 'Oh well, let's be different for once. Off you go!'

Mum had carefully laid the day's clothes out for them so it didn't take Lucy long to get herself into her school uniform. She needed help with her top shirt button and her tie. Dad was brilliant at doing ties. Mum's ties were usually a bit wonky.

Then Lucy went to the bathroom and dutifully scrubbed her teeth while Dad tried to coax Michael into his clothes.

Michael would never stand still. Mum had got very good at dressing him while chasing him round the bedroom, but Dad was usually walking the dog while this went on, so he was new to the sport. At the moment, Michael had the upper hand.

Since Dad wasn't watching her, Lucy decided not to bother with a wash. Her face looked clean enough. Washing was really boring.

Just then, Dad walked into the bathroom with Michael tucked under one arm.

'OK, Lucy?' he asked.

'Yes, fine,' Lucy replied. Her eye fell on the bottle of mouthwash that Mum always put on top of the bathroom cabinet. She did that to keep it out of Michael's way.

'Could I have some mouthwash please, Dad?' she asked. She loved the tingly, minty feeling it left in her mouth.

'Yes, of course!' smiled Dad. He lifted the bottle down.

'Mikey want to give it to Lucy!' piped up Michael.

'What a kind boy!' said Dad, handing the bottle to Michael.

'Er, Dad, I'm not sure that's—' began Lucy. She was about to say 'a good idea' because she knew what her little brother could be like. But before she could finish her sentence, Michael threw the bottle at her. Somehow the top came off and Lucy got drenched in bright blue mouthwash!

Oh Dad!

Michael squealed with laughter.

'Oh Dad!' exclaimed Lucy. 'Look what Michael's done. My uniform's soaking.'

'Oh golly!' gasped Dad, quickly plonking Michael down. He grabbed a towel and started to dab Lucy's clothes, but that did no good. The blue stain was spreading. Then he put water on the towel and scrubbed Lucy's uniform like mad. That only seemed to spread the stain even further.

'I can't go to school like this!' wailed Lucy. Then she added, hopefully, 'I'll have to stay at home.'

'Don't be silly,' said Dad. 'There must be a spare uniform for you somewhere – mustn't there?'

Lucy shook her head. 'No, I grew out of the other pinafore, and my spare white blouse is missing three buttons. Mum's been meaning to sew them on for ages but she keeps forgetting.'

'Well, what about that green suit thing you wear sometimes,' suggested Dad, desperately.

'Suit thing?' echoed Lucy. 'Oh, my tracksuit! But that's only for games day. Games day is Monday, Dad. Today is Thursday.'

'You'll have to wear it today, love,' sighed Dad. 'You can't go to school as you are. Let's see if we can find it.'

15

'But Dad,' whined Lucy, 'everyone will think I'm stupid for wearing my tracksuit on the wrong day.'

'Never mind what they think!' snapped Dad. 'Hurry up and get changed. We've got a bus to catch.'

They found Lucy's tracksuit in the dirty washing pile. Luckily it was only a little bit grubby so Lucy quickly changed into it.

'I'll write a note for your teacher explaining why you're in your games kit, shall I?' offered Dad. 'What's her name again? Mrs Paddock, isn't it?'

'No, Dad, it's Mrs Pollock,' Lucy corrected him. 'And please will you wash my uniform today? I must have it tomorrow.'

'I will!' promised Dad, trotting after Michael and trying to get a jumper over his head. 'Go and find your shoes, and then we must be off. Now, Mikey, please stay still!'

Lucy stomped downstairs. Honestly, what

a start to the day, she thought grumpily. Trudy Taylor would make fun of her all day because she was in her games uniform. And Andy Murphy would think she was stupid. She so wanted Andy Murphy not to think she was stupid. She really liked Andy Murphy.

Lucy sighed as she pulled her runners on and stuck the velcro straps down firmly. It was going to be a rotten day, and it was all Dad's fault. Mum would never let Michael throw mouthwash over her.

She sat sulking on the stairs until she heard Dad clumping down behind her.

'Come on, Pumpkin,' he called. 'Get your coat and rucksack. We need to head off. Mikey, stop wriggling!'

He had Michael firmly clamped under his arm and was pulling on the last sock. With impressive speed, he pulled Michael's raincoat on and shoved his feet into his wellington boots.

'Wrong feet!' Michael pointed out crossly.

'Oh, never mind for now,' said Dad, distractedly. He was battling with the buggy. It was refusing to open.

'Come on, stupid thing,' he muttered crossly, shaking it. But the buggy still wouldn't open.

'Oh, Dad!' sighed Lucy. 'You haven't undone the safety clip. Look.'

She deftly lifted the little red hook that Dad had missed.

'Oh, thanks,' grinned Dad. 'Silly me. Now come along, we've got to run.'

They hurried out of the front door and down the hill. Dad was taking big paces. Lucy couldn't keep up.

'Hey, wait for me!' she panted. Dad slowed down.

'Come on, I'll give you a piggy back!' he offered, bending down in front of her.

She jumped up onto his back and grabbed on to his big, strong shoulders. Dad set off again, bumping Lucy about. It was really fun! Lucy giggled. She was about to forgive Dad for the morning's disasters when she suddenly realised she hadn't got her lunch.

'Dad, my lunch!' she cried.

'What?' Dad stopped in his tracks.

Lucy slid off his back and looked at him accusingly.

'Oh, Dad, you never made me any lunch!'

'Was I meant to?' asked Dad.

'Yes, Mum told you to get my lunch this morning. I heard her,' pouted Lucy.

'Oh dear, I am sorry, Pumpkin,' sighed Dad. 'But look, there's the bus coming now. I'll drop some lunch down to the school for you later, after I've taken Michael to play-school. I'll put some extra treats in too, OK?'

Lucy nodded. She liked the sound of the treats!

Chapter 2
A Hungry Day

As soon as she got on the bus, the teasing began.

'Lucy thinks it's Monday!' sneered Brian Feeney. Several girls giggled at her. Lucy glowered. What a rotten day it was. Hurry up and come home, Mum, she pleaded silently.

She was still seething at morning break. Dad hadn't turned up with her lunch yet, and she was starving. She always had something to eat at morning break. She didn't want to admit to anyone that she'd forgotten her lunch. That on top of having the wrong uniform on was really uncool.

So she skulked in a corner of the yard. She didn't see Dad coming in. But he caught sight of her.

21

'Cooee! Pumpkin!' he shouted, walking briskly towards her.

Lucy froze when she heard his voice ring out. A hush fell over the yard, as everyone turned to see who Pumpkin was. For a moment Lucy wondered about pretending that he wasn't her Dad. But then Dad called out, 'Lucy! Here's your lunch!'

She had no choice but to turn round. Dad held the lunch box out with a flourish. Lucy nearly died! Dad was holding out Michael's Teletubbies lunch box, not her Barbie one.

That was even worse than him calling her Pumpkin!

'Oh, Dad!' she hissed, her face red with embarrassment. 'That's not my lunch box!'

As she took the lunch box in her hands Lucy hoped against hope that Andy Murphy wasn't looking.

'You know, I didn't think it was, but Mikey insisted the Barbie one was his, so I let him have it. Anyway, it doesn't matter that much, does it?' smiled Dad.

Oh Dad! Lucy groaned to herself. How could Dad even *think* it didn't matter?

'Just wait till you see what's in it. That'll cheer you up! See you later.' Dad turned to go and Lucy was left standing with a Teletubbies lunch box clutched to her chest.

The sniggering began at once.

'Lucy's a pumpkin, a big, fat pumpkin!'

'Lucy loves the Teletubbies! Uh-oh!'

'Pumpkin, pumpkin, Lucy lumpkin.'

'Shut up!' snarled Lucy at the gang of boys who were teasing her, but they just laughed.

She stormed off to another part of the yard where Miss Kenny, one of the teachers, was on yard duty. The boys wouldn't dare to be rude to Lucy there.

Lucy opened her lunch box – and gasped! It was crammed full of goodies: two packets of crisps, a bar of chocolate, a can of fizzy orange, a packet of chewing gum and a lollipop. But they were all things they weren't allowed to have at school. Lucy slammed the lid shut, but not before Miss Kenny had seen what was inside.

'Now, Lucy, you'd better give me your lunch box. You know you aren't allowed to have crisps and sweets and fizzy drinks at school, don't you?' she snapped severely.

Lucy nodded and sadly handed over the lunch box.

'Yes, Miss Kenny,' Lucy muttered.

Lucy knew the rules and Mum knew the rules, but Dad obviously didn't. Oh Dad! You've done it again, Lucy thought bitterly.

'You can collect this from me when you go home this afternoon. I'm sure one of your friends will share their lunch with you. You can always go and ask for some biscuits at the staff room if you like,' said Miss Kenny.

Lucy decided she'd rather starve than beg for biscuits off the teachers. She stomped off again, almost in tears, ignoring the giggling and taunts that followed her.

The rest of the day dragged on dismally. Angela Hughes gave her a soggy cheese sandwich at lunchtime which tasted disgusting.

Lots of the boys offered her slices of imaginary pumpkin pie!

It seemed an age before the bell for the end of school went. Lucy went to collect her lunch box. Miss Kenny gave her another lecture about what she was and was not allowed to have for lunch.

Lucy had to bite her tongue to stop her saying something rude to Miss Kenny. It wasn't *her* fault, it was her silly Dad's!

Lucy didn't get the bus home in the evenings so she dawdled – as slowly as she could – to the school gate to wait to be collected. She'd make Dad have to wait for her as a punishment. Only Dad wasn't there! Lucy scanned the line of Mums and Dads waiting across the road. She saw Mrs Patel in a beautiful sari. She saw Robert's mum, Mrs Brown, in an elegant suit. And there was Colin's Mum in a lovely bright outfit as usual.

But no sign of Dad.

Lucy waited inside the gate. She waited and waited. All the other children filed out past her, giving her pitying looks. No one liked being the last one home. Soon everyone had gone. There was just Lucy and the school warden, who kept muttering and looking at her watch. Lucy fumed quietly while her tummy rumbled loudly.

Then, at last, Lucy caught sight of a figure jogging up the hill. It was Dad! He came puffing up to the crossing. The school warden hurried Lucy across and then went to get changed out of her big white coat and yellow jacket.

'Dad! Where have you been?' exploded Lucy. 'I've been waiting for hours!'

'Sorry, love,' panted Dad, giving her a hug. 'I forgot the time. I thought you came out at twenty past three instead of ten past. I really am sorry. How was your lunch? I bet you enjoyed it today.'

As they wandered back down the hill to the car, Lucy explained that they weren't allowed crisps, chewing gum, sweets and fizzy drinks at school.

'What a rotten lot they are!' protested Dad. 'Poor love, you must be hungry. Never mind, we'll be home soon.'

Lucy climbed into the car next to a sleeping Michael. Dad chatted away but Lucy didn't really listen. She was too busy feeling sorry for herself.

Chapter 3
What's Cooking?

'Here we are,' Dad said, pulling up outside the front door. 'Let's have tea. Michael and I found some lovely buns in the cake tin. We saved some for you.'

'Nice buns,' said Michael, now awake.

Lucy stopped moping at once.

'What? The cake tin? The one at the back of the food cupboard?' she demanded.

'That's the one!' beamed Dad.

'Oh Dad!' cried Lucy. 'They were the buns Mum and I made yesterday for the Beavers' cake sale tonight. You weren't meant to eat them.'

'Oh heck,' groaned Dad, 'I didn't realise. Nobody tells me anything. I guess I'll have to help you make some more.'

'Actually, we might not need to,' Lucy informed him. 'Mum and I made a lovely iced walnut cake as well. That's in the fridge.'

'Um, it *was* in the fridge,' admitted Dad sheepishly. 'Most of it is in Michael and me now!'

'Oh no!' Lucy wailed. 'You've eaten that too? Oh Dad!'

Lucy hurtled through the front door which Dad had just opened, ran upstairs and flung herself on her bed. She heard Dad calling but she ignored him. She knew it was rude but she was really, really fed up.

Presently she heard the clank of baking tins in the kitchen and Michael shout 'hoorah!' Then she heard Dad rummaging in the food cupboard. Finally she heard a glass object fall onto the floor with a smash followed by Dad muttering angrily. Then she heard the hum of the vacuum cleaner.

Next she heard her tummy rumble. She was so busy moping she'd forgotten how hungry she was. She decided to go and help Dad do some baking. She'd get to lick the bowl that way.

'Hi Dad!' she said cheerfully, standing at the doorway of the kitchen.

'Hi there,' he replied, looking very relieved at seeing her. 'Please come and help. I'm hopeless at baking. I don't suppose your Beavers would like a nice curry instead.'

'It's a cake sale so no curries allowed,' smiled Lucy. 'And anyway, there's no such thing as a nice curry.'

'Rubbish!' snorted Dad. 'Well, boring old buns it is then. I'll put Mikey down for a sleep and we'll get stuck in.'

Lucy and Dad worked away happily. Lucy licked the spoon to test the mixture.

'More sugar,' she ordered. Dad shovelled some more sugar in.

Lucy licked again. 'And some more.'

'Sure?' asked Dad. Lucy nodded wisely. Dad shrugged and emptied the rest of the packet into the bowl. 'How's that?'

'Hmm, not bad. I reckon it could do with some golden syrup now.'

'That's not in the recipe,' Dad pointed out, taking a quick peek at the cookery book.

'I still think it needs it,' said Lucy.

Dad obediently added several large dollops of golden syrup.

'Looks a bit sticky to me,' he said, peering into the bowl.

'Better put some more flour in then,' Lucy advised him.

'Okey-dokey,' said Dad and tipped some more flour out of the bag.

It all came out in a rush and Lucy and Dad disappeared in a cloud of flour for a moment.

Lucy sneezed loudly. 'Not that much!' she protested.

'Whoops, my mistake,' apologised Dad. 'Now, how does that taste?'

Lucy licked the spoon again.

'Not bad. It just needs some currants to finish it off.'

Dad threw in several generous handfuls of currants. Lucy took one more lick.

'Perfect!' she announced.

'What shall we cook it in?' asked Dad, gesturing to the pile of baking trays and cake tins of different shapes and sizes.

'Hmm, this one I think!' said Lucy, choosing a large, square cake tin.

'OK,' said Dad.

He and Lucy half poured and half scraped the very sticky mixture into the tin. It sat in a sad-looking heap in the middle of the tin.

'It looks a bit lost in there,' observed Dad.

'Don't worry, it'll spread out while it cooks,' Lucy reassured him.

'I'm sure it will,' agreed Dad. 'Let's put it on to cook and go and get the washing out of the tumble dryer. Your uniform will be as good as new now.'

Dad shoved the cake tin into the oven and turned it on at a nice high setting. Lucy went into the utility room to deal with the clothes. She pulled open the tumble dryer door and fished out her green cardigan.

Dad was right – it did look as good as new, all nice and clean again. She gave it a shake – and gasped with horror. Her cardigan had shrunk – and shrunk and shrunk! It wouldn't even fit Michael now.

She was about to yell to Dad to come and see when she caught sight of a strange green blouse in the tumble dryer that she'd never seen before. She bent down and pulled it out. Her heart sank. It wasn't a new green blouse at all. It was her old white one that had turned green in the wash.

'Oh, Dad!' she groaned. 'You've done it again.'

Chapter 4
Smoke Gets in your Eyes

She carried the garments into the kitchen and mournfully held them out.

'Ah!' said Dad, and scratched his head. 'Problem. I guess I shouldn't have used such a hot wash for them should I?'

Lucy shook her head sorrowfully.

'And you're not having an extra games day tomorrow by any chance?' he asked hopefully.

Lucy shook her head again.

'OK,' he sighed. 'I'll get Michael up and we'll nip into town and get you a new uniform.'

They were ages in town. They found a new white blouse quickly enough, but had to try several shops to find a green cardigan.

It was hard to find the right shade for school. It was after six o'clock when they got back home.

'Goodness, what a busy day!' said Dad as he unlocked the front door and pushed it open. A cloud of smoke billowed out into their faces. They could hear the mad beep-beeping of the smoke alarm in the kitchen.

'Oh, Dad!' cried Lucy. 'The house is on fire!'

'No, I don't think it's the house – just our cake. I completely forgot we'd left it cooking in the oven. Wait here, I'll go and turn the oven off.'

Dad disappeared into the smoke-filled kitchen. He returned a few moments later brandishing the cake tin with his hands in oven mitts. It was trailing a cloud of black smoke and smelled terrible. Dad hurled it onto the lawn. He opened and closed the front door about twenty times to help the smoke out of the house.

'It's really smelly in there,' he informed Lucy and Michael. 'We'll just have to grab what we need for Beavers and get some tea on the way. If I leave some windows open, the smoke and smell should all have gone by the time we get back. Golly, your Mum's going to murder me!'

Lucy felt a bit like murdering Dad too as she rushed upstairs to change for Beavers.

She still had no buns to take to the cake sale. She'd be the only one who didn't bring anything. She sighed as she quickly pulled on her jumper and trousers, both of which smelt of burnt cooking. That wasn't surprising since the whole house smelt of burnt cooking. She rolled her neckerchief and fastened the woggle up around it. They too smelled horrid.

She pulled her black shoes on and ran downstairs. Dad had grabbed Michael's changing bag, everyone's coats and a couple of paper plates.

'Let's find some tea quickly. We can call by the garage near the Scout Hall and buy some buns for you to take, Lucy. If you take them out of the plastic wrappers and put them on these plates, no one will know you didn't make them yourself.'

'Gosh, that's sneaky, Dad,' said Lucy, admiringly.

They set off and drove to the Indian takeaway. Lucy groaned.

'I don't like curry!' she reminded Dad.

'Mikey no like curry!' added Michael.

'I know, I know,' soothed Dad. 'I'll get chips for you two, but I must say I fancy something really hot and spicy after all our adventures. I think I'll have a pork vindaloo.'

Lucy and Michael waited in the car while Dad went to get the food. He was back five minutes later with three steaming packages. Lucy cheered up as she unwrapped a mound of piping hot chips.

She smiled happily as she tucked in.

Michael was happy too as he played with his chips, dropping lots of them onto the car seat and the floor.

But Dad wasn't so content. His vindaloo was a lot hotter than he'd expected!

'Oh, ah, ah, phew!' he spluttered after a mouthful, flapping his hands in front of his open mouth. 'My mouth's on fire!'

'Oh Dad!' laughed Lucy. 'You are silly!'

'I need some coke quick!' exclaimed Dad, starting the engine and driving to the garage. He dashed in and came back with two cans of coke and several packets of chocolate buns.

'Here you are, Pumpkin!' he said, throwing the buns to Lucy. 'Pop them on those plates and no one will be any the wiser.'

Lucy grinned wickedly as she followed Dad's instructions. Then she quickly finished her chips while Dad drove on to the Scout Hall where the Beavers were having the cake sale. They were late – of course.

Chapter 5
Dad to the Rescue

They could hear quite a commotion going on as they walked up to the Scout Hall.

'Goodness,' said Dad, 'I didn't know cake sales were so rowdy!'

But when they opened the door to go in they soon saw what all the fuss was about. Two long trestle tables were spread with delicious cakes and buns of every description. But there were also two huge, mean-looking dogs helping themselves to everything on display!

The Beaver leader and several mums were nervously trying to shoo the dogs away, but the animals weren't taking any notice. However, if anyone tried to come too close, they would growl menacingly.

43

The Beavers were in a huddle together near the doorway, whispering in scared voices. There was a huddle of mums too.

'Good heavens, whose pets are those?' Dad asked one of the twittering mums.

'They're strays,' she explained. 'They followed one of the Beavers in and we can't get rid of them. They seem to be ravenous. They're eating everything in sight!'

'They're ravenous, are they?' said Dad, thoughtfully. 'And eating everything!' He winked at Lucy and shot out of the hall.

'Hmm, he's not much help, is he?' sniffed one mum. Lucy, sadly, had to agree with her. But then Dad reappeared with his uneaten pork vindaloo.

He marched up to the dogs. They turned away from the dainty pink fairy cakes they were currently demolishing and growled at him, their hackles raised.

'You don't scare me,' Dad said breezily.

'Now, here's something you'll love, guys. You don't want to bother with all that sissy stuff!' He waved his arm at the delicate buns and cakes. 'Here's something *real* dogs eat.' He held out the curry. The dogs looked at him warily.

Lucy held her breath. So did everyone else.

'Good dogs! Nice dogs!' coaxed Dad as he carefully laid the carton of vindaloo on the floor just in front of the dogs. It certainly smelt quite nice, all rich and spicy.

The dogs sniffed it closely. Then one decided to take a large mouthful. Not wanting to be left out, his companion took a huge gulp as well.

Lucy could see the expressions on the dogs' faces change from delight to horror as the force of the vindaloo hit them. The first dog let out a strangled howl while the other dog began coughing and sneezing violently. They both took one last terrified look at Dad – the person who had caused them so much suffering – and then fled from the hall, tails firmly between their legs.

There was a stunned silence in the hall for a few seconds. Then all the Beavers cheered and the Beaver leader stepped forward and shook Dad's hand.

'Thanks a million!' she gushed gratefully. 'Those dogs would have eaten everything if you hadn't got rid of them.'

'It was nothing!' shrugged Dad modestly.

'Yes, well done, Lucy's dad!' cried some of the Beavers.

'Lucy, you never told us what a clever dad you had!' the Beaver leader accused her.

That, thought Lucy, rather ashamed, is because I didn't realise myself.

'Oh Dad!' she said out loud. 'Well done!' And she gave him a gigantic hug.

Mum was away for another day and Lucy didn't doubt for an instant that tomorrow would be as full of mishap and muddle as today had been, but suddenly she didn't care.

Dad had saved the day. He was really, really cool. Oh Dad!

48